# KLONDY *and the* WOLF DOG

## by Susan McCloskey • illustrated by Tim Scoggins

## Harcourt

Orlando   Boston   Dallas   Chicago   San Diego

*Visit The Learning Site!*

**www.harcourtschool.com**

There he was again. Klondy watched from the doorway of her cabin as the animal burrowed his nose in the snow, digging fiercely with his front feet at the same time. He was on the hunt, that was for sure, but the animal had no luck this time. Whatever small creature he had scented had scampered away.

The animal looked up from his digging and turned his gaze toward Klondy. Then he tossed his head and gave a snort to clear the snow from his nostrils. Klondy smiled. Although he had a lot of the wolf in him, the gesture made him look just like a big, playful dog.

2

"Water's boiling, Klondy!" Papa's weak voice came from inside the cabin. Startled, the wolf dog ran away. His white fur blended so well with the snow that Klondy could scarcely tell in which direction he ran.

Klondy turned from the doorway. "Coming, Papa!" she answered. Better not to tell Papa she had seen the wolf dog, she told herself. He'd worry if he knew that the beast had been so close to the cabin, and Papa had enough to worry about.

"How are you feeling, Papa?" Klondy felt Papa's damp forehead.

"Not quite ready to prospect yet," Papa said with difficulty. He attempted to smile at Klondy, but she could see that his heart wasn't in it. Not for the first time, she missed the sparkle that used to light up his dark brown eyes.

Papa had been sick since the beginning of winter. He had tried to go ice fishing before the river had frozen solid—"like a crazy fool," he said later—and had fallen through the ice into frigid water up to his neck. Fortunately, Klondy had been setting up a rabbit snare nearby and had heard his cries for help. If she had been inside the cabin instead of outside when it happened, things would be very different now.

Lying flat on the ice to distribute her weight, Klondy had extended a tree limb to Papa and had managed to pull him out. She was just in time. If the rescue had taken any longer, he wouldn't have had the strength to hang on.

The name of the river Papa had fallen into was the Klondike, and ever since she rescued him, that was Papa's name for her, too. Klondy for short. It was a funny thing, but she had stopped thinking of herself as Susannah. Klondy seemed like a more fitting name for a girl who was living in the Yukon.

Papa's dunking in the Klondike had given him a cold and fever that had never improved and were now getting worse, thanks to the long, bitter winter.

Thoughts of the endless winter prompted Klondy to declare, "Spring is coming soon, Papa!" as she helped him sit up to drink his tea. She chatted on as she settled down with some sewing. "The first thing I'm going to do when the weather warms up is get rid of all the old moss." Klondy was talking about the thick moss they used to plug the cracks between the logs of the cabin. It did a good job of keeping the cold winds out, but it was a breeding ground for insects. Klondy knew that if she tarried long in getting rid of it, the bugs that hatched would make life miserable in the summer.

"What about you, Papa? What are you going to do come spring?"

Especially since his illness, Klondy often tried to engage Papa in talk about spring. Recently it was all that interested him. Spring meant that the river would thaw, and that meant he could get on with his search for gold. It also meant that the boats from Washington could get through. Surely one of them would bring a letter from Mama, who had stayed home in Washington with Klondy's baby brother, Ezra.

Klondy had asked the same question before, and it had always prompted Papa to launch into a list of all the chores that needed to be done before the prospecting season: build new sluice boxes, make sure the shovels and pickaxes were in good repair, and buy a mule to replace the one that he had retired after it had injured its leg. This time, however, Papa didn't say anything.

Klondy looked up from her sewing. Papa was staring out the window, so she stood up and followed his gaze. There was the wolf dog. He was standing where she had observed him previously, staring at the cabin.

Suddenly Papa was trying to throw off his heavy blankets. "Papa! Papa!" Klondy said loudly, putting her hand on his shoulder to restrain him. "You stay in bed! I'll make him go away."

6

Klondy ran from the cabin, waving her arms. "Go away! Stay out of here!" she shouted. The wolf dog immediately scampered off, and Klondy returned to her father's side.

"He's gone, Papa. Don't worry," she said, helping him lie back down.

"I wish that dog would stay away," he muttered.

Klondy wiped the sweat from Papa's forehead. His fever had gotten worse. Klondy had noticed that the weaker Papa became, the more the wolf dog agitated him. Was it because he realized that he was unable to protect her from the wild animal?

The dog had first appeared toward the end of the summer. About a month earlier, Klondy and Papa had arrived in Dawson, joining thousands of others who had already made the long journey to the Yukon Territory of Canada, hoping to strike it rich after gold was discovered there. They had hired a boat to take them up the Klondike River to a small abandoned claim Papa had heard about. The earlier prospector's tiny log cabin still stood near the riverbank.

As he helped Klondy and Papa unload their belongings, the boatman said, "They say the last fellow who lived here left a dog behind—a huge, white, scary thing. I'd be real careful of him if I were you. If he's still alive, he's wild as a wolf by now."

So Klondy wasn't completely surprised the first time she
saw the wolf dog. She and Papa were out chopping spruce
boughs to cover the narrow bunks they slept in. Klondy had
just spied a blueberry bush that she had missed on her earlier
outings. It was laden with ripe, juicy berries.

"Papa!" she called. "I found some more berries! I'm going
back to get my bucket!" Dragging the spruce boughs behind
her, Klondy hiked back home.

She had just left the woods and was headed up the wind-
ing trail to the cabin. She looked ahead, and there he was—a
big white dog, or maybe a wolf, sitting alertly in front of the
door as if he was waiting for someone to come home and let
him in.

8

Klondy stopped and stared
at the animal. The wolf dog's tail
began to wag slightly, and he
opened his mouth in a wide, eager
grin.

Klondy took a step toward him. Just
then a hand gently grasped her arm from
behind.

"Don't take another step!" Papa warned in a
whisper. "Remember what the boatman said.
That dog is as wild as a wolf. He might look tame,
but he can't be trusted!"

Then Papa abruptly stepped in front of Klondy
and began shouting harshly at the animal.

"Get going! Stay away from here!" The startled
beast ran off, with Papa chasing after it, waving
one of the spruce branches he had been dragging
behind him.

After that day, Papa forbade Klondy to leave the cabin by herself. That's how he had been back then—cautious of an animal he felt was wild and unpredictable. After he got sick, though, his caution seemed to become fear. Now just the sight of the animal agitated him so much that he had Klondy worried. It made her realize just how much he was suffering. She had to get a doctor.

As soon as the thought entered her mind, Klondy scoffed at herself. *Get* a doctor? Where did she think she was, back in the city? No. She had to transport Papa *to* a doctor. That meant getting him to Dawson, ten miles away. She would have to use the old sled that was stored behind the cabin.

Papa had fallen into a restless sleep. Klondy paced around the cabin, gathering her energy and preparing for the long, frigid, and dangerous journey ahead.

10

Within an
hour, they were heading
south. Covered in caribou skins,
Papa lay on the sled, which Klondy pulled
over the packed snow. Her thick clothing and caribou
parka added to her bulk, and she resembled a small
brown bear.

The sliver of daylight that appeared every day of the arctic winter had long passed, but the snow shone under a full moon. Suddenly Klondy pointed toward the sky.

"Look, Papa!" she said. A shimmering canopy of red, yellow, blue, and green light was spreading over the dark sky. It was the aurora borealis—the northern lights.

Klondy glanced back to see whether Papa was aware of the lights, and his smile showed that he was. Then Klondy saw something else. It was the wolf dog, following them.

11

Klondy was frightened.
Previously, when she had seen the
animal, she had been close to the cabin and
safety, but not this time.

Klondy didn't dare tell Papa. She wanted to keep him as calm as possible. She was on her own.

What could the animal want? she wondered. Was he hungry? Suddenly she remembered the food she was carrying, the dried salmon and cold sourdough pancakes she had stuffed inside her parka. That must be it! The wolf dog was following the scent of the salmon. If she got rid of it, he would eat it and wander away.

Checking that Papa was sleeping, Klondy took out the packet of food and flung it at the wolf dog. The salmon and pancakes scattered on the snow, and in no time, the beast had gobbled up every morsel. Then he kept on following.

Much later, Klondy looked back. The wolf dog was still following, although he hadn't come any closer. It was as if he was intentionally keeping out of Papa's sight.

Now Klondy was worried about the weather. Gradually, clouds had covered the moon, and the sky became pitch black.

"We have to stop, Papa," she said. "I can't see where we're going."

After a struggle, Klondy managed to disengage herself from the sled. She assisted Papa in getting up, and together they spread a caribou skin on the snow. By feel alone she mounded snow at one end of the skin and rested one end of the overturned sled on it. Two caribou skins thrown over the top and sides of the sled completed the shelter.

With Klondy's help, Papa crawled under the sled, and she covered him with the last caribou skin. As she crawled in beside him, she thought about the wolf dog. Where was he? It was too dark to tell, but she hoped he had finally gone away. Then, like Papa, she immediately fell asleep.

A short while later, Klondy woke up shivering. A howling wind swept through their makeshift shelter, and drifts of snow blew in. As she huddled beside Papa, Klondy felt herself grow colder and colder. Klondy became worried that, because he was so weak, Papa must be colder still. What if this trip makes him even sicker? she wondered.

Then Klondy heard something. At first she thought it was the wind, but then she realized it was a whine. She prayed Papa hadn't heard. Then the whining grew louder.

"Klondy," Papa whispered. He paused.
Then he said, "Best let that dog in.
We'll freeze if we don't."

When Klondy woke up, she was as warm as toast.

In the thin light that seeped through the cracks in the shelter, she could see the wolf dog, flopped between her and Papa, with his big head on Papa's chest.

Papa turned his head to look at her. "Daylight, Klondy," he said. "I think my fever has broken. Time to get going." The wolf dog scrambled up.

After they had taken down the shelter, Papa rested in the sled while he gave advice on how to fit the harness to the dog. Soon they were off, the dog trotting briskly because his load was light.

"Papa," Klondy said "we're going to make it to Dawson. We're going to get help, and you're going to get better!"

Papa smiled, and this time Klondy saw light in his eyes.

Then, with a sly smile, Papa said pointedly, "I sure could do with some dried salmon and sourdough pancakes, though."

Surprised, Klondy said, "I thought you were asleep when I threw them out!"

"I figured out exactly what you were doing," Papa said. "I decided there was nothing to do but lie low and hope for the best. It sure seemed like you were making the right decisions at every turn." He went on as he watched the dog pulling strongly, "The dog's making good use of his meal! We'll make sure he eats well when we get to Dawson. He'll need the strength."

The wolf dog looked back at them as if he knew what Papa meant. He would need strength for the return trip home—home to their cabin on the Klondike.